KT-513-244

...ulele
Liam

by Lucinda Cotter

C334042268

a Capstone company — publishers for children

Engage Literacy is published in the UK by Raintree.
Raintree is an imprint of Capstone Global Library Limited, a company incorporated in England and Wales
having its registered office at 264 Banbury Road, Oxford, OX2 7DY – Registered company number: 6695582

www.raintree.co.uk

© 2017 by Raintree. All rights reserved. No part of this publication may be reproduced, stored in a retrieval
system, or transmitted in any way or by any means, electronic, mechanical, photocopying, recording or
otherwise, without the prior written permission of Capstone Global Library Limited.

Text copyright © Capstone 2017

Illustration copyright © Capstone/Angie Jones

Editorial credits
Gina Kammer, editor; Charmaine Whitman, designer; Tori Abraham, production specialist

10 9 8 7 6 5 4 3 2 1
Printed and bound in China.

Ukulele Liam

ISBN: 978-1-4747-3161-4

Contents

Chapter 1
Liam's tiny guitar

"Hey, Dad!" said Liam. "I've just learned a new song on my ukulele. I'm playing it in front of my class tomorrow. Would you like to hear it?"

Dad looked up from his computer as he stopped typing. "Of course," he smiled. "I'd love to hear it!"

Liam's aunt had given him a ukulele for his birthday. She had also helped him learn how to play it. Liam had been practising every day, and he could already play quite a few songs. He strummed the strings of the ukulele over and over.

When Liam was finished, Dad clapped loudly. "Wow! That was great!" he said excitedly. "You're getting really good at playing that tiny guitar, aren't you?"

Liam frowned at Dad. "It's not a tiny guitar. It's a full-size ukulele. It's meant to be this small."

"I know," grinned Dad. "I was only joking. And you play it really well. I bet your class will think so, too."

Chapter 2
Not funny

At school, Liam got ready to play his ukulele for his class. He was so nervous his knees were shaking. He'd never had people listen to him before, apart from Dad. Even so, he played a whole song without making a mistake. Everyone in the class clapped.

"Bravo!" said Ms Tang, his teacher. "That was wonderful, Liam."

Liam was happy it was all over. He had performed well, and everyone seemed to enjoy his playing.

But at break time, near the playground, Liam saw Tanya and her friends pointing and laughing at him.

When he walked past them, Tanya called out to him. "Hey, Liam! How did your guitar shrink? Did you put it in the wash by mistake?" She put her hands on her hips. "It looks like it was made for a baby. Are you a baby, Liam? You must be if you play a baby guitar like that."

Tanya's friends laughed and pretended to be babies, but Liam didn't find it funny.

Every time Tanya saw Liam from then on, she laughed at him.

"Maybe Dad was right," thought Liam, "and the ukulele really is just a stupid, tiny guitar."

Liam didn't feel like playing it much after that.

When Dad asked Liam why he wasn't practising his ukulele, Liam made up different stories:

"I hurt my hand playing basketball," he said the first day.

"I've got too much homework to do," he said the next day.

"One of the strings is broken," he said after that, and then Dad stopped asking.

But the truth was, Liam didn't want to be teased.

When Ms Tang asked him if he would play in front of the whole school, Liam shook his head. "Sorry, Ms Tang. I don't think I can do it."

Ms Tang could see that something was wrong. "I understand if you feel nervous about playing in front of so many people," she said.

"That isn't the reason," said Liam. "I've decided to give up playing the ukulele."

"But why?" asked Ms Tang. "You play it so well."

"It's a stupid instrument," Liam replied angrily. "Ukuleles are for babies."

Chapter 3
A ukulele surprise

A few weeks later, Ms Tang had a surprise for her class. "Today, we have some visitors to our school," she said. "They are members of a very special band, and they are going to play for us."

Liam couldn't believe his eyes when the members of the band came walking into the classroom. They were all carrying ukuleles!

"Please give a big welcome to the Ukulele Youth Band," smiled Ms Tang, and everyone cheered.

Some of the ukuleles in the band were just like Liam's ukulele, and some were even smaller.

But to Liam's surprise, some of the ukuleles were bigger than his. There was one that was the same size as a guitar!

"As you can see, ukuleles come in many sizes," said Ms Tang. "There is a tiny pocket ukulele, right up to a giant ukulele, which is called a bass ukulele. Playing any of them takes practice and skill."

The boy with the bass ukulele plucked the strings, and it made a deep, hollow sound. Liam was amazed.

Then the band began to play, and music filled the classroom.

They strummed and they plucked, and sometimes they sang. They even asked the pupils to join in and sing along.

It was the best music Liam had ever heard, and he couldn't keep his fingers still. They wanted to join in and strum along with the band.

The clapping after the concert was very loud, so Liam knew the other children must have enjoyed it, too.

Chapter 4
A change of heart

When Liam got home from school, he took his ukulele out of its case and played a song. He played song, after song, after song. It felt so good to make music again.

"Hey! I've missed that sound," grinned Dad. "You must have finally got that broken string fixed, then?"

"Something like that," Liam smiled back.

The next day at school, Liam spoke to Ms Tang. "If you still want me to play for our school, I think I can do it now," he said.

"That's wonderful news, Liam," replied Ms Tang. "I'm so glad you've decided to play the ukulele again."

At lunchtime, Liam saw Tanya with her group of friends. They were all around her, looking at something.

As Liam got closer, he saw that Tanya was playing a ukulele! But from what he could hear, she wasn't doing very well.

"Hey, Liam!" she called to him.

He waited to hear what terrible thing she would say to him this time. But to his surprise, she came running over with her ukulele. She told Liam she was sorry for teasing him.

"This belonged to my dad," said Tanya. "He gave it to me. It's not as good as yours, but I was hoping you could teach me to play it."

"Of course," replied Liam. He took the ukulele and gave it a strum. "It's not bad." Then he smiled at Tanya and said, "Did this guitar shrink in the wash, too?"